KNOCK! KNOCK!

By Jackie Carter

Illustrated by Nancy Poydar

SCHOLASTIC INC.
NEW YORK TORONTO LONDON AUCKLAND SYDNEY

Library of Congress Cataloging-in-Publication Data

Carter, Jackie, date.
    Knock! knock! / by Jackie Carter; illustrated by
Nancy Poydar.
        p. cm. — (My first library)
    Summary: A mother and daughter receive a flurry
of surprise guests at their new home.
    ISBN 0-590-49335-3   ISBN 0-590-29263-3 (meets NASTA specifications)
    [1. Moving, Household—Fiction. 2. Stories in rhyme.]
I. Poydar, Nancy, ill. II. Title. III. Series.
PZ8.3.C247Kn 1993
[E]—dc20   92-44631
                           CIP
                           AC

Copyright © 1993 by Scholastic Inc.
Illustrations copyright © 1993 Nancy Poydar
Designed by Bill SMITH STUDIO, Inc.
All rights reserved. Published by Scholastic Inc.
My First Library is a trademark of Scholastic Inc.
    4 5 6 7 8 9 10   09   01 00 99 98 97 96 95
Printed in the U.S.A.
First Scholastic printing, 1993

*To Jack, whose door
was always open.
J.C.*

In our new house at half-past four,
We heard some knock-knocks at our door.

 The knocks woke up our dog, Sinclair.
Knock-knock! We asked the knocks,
"Who's there?"

No answer came. Not one reply.
And then my mother caught my eye.
"Before we see about those knocks,
I'll find my shoes. You find your socks."

6

While searching almost everywhere
For shoes and socks that were not there,
Inside, outside every box,
Our new front door knocked two more...

7

KNOCKS!

9

"Be right there," my mother said.
She looked at me. I scratched my head.
I wondered too, who could this be?
Someone for Mom? Someone for me?

Mom got up. I got up too.
Mom could only find one shoe.
With one foot wearing just a sock,
She walked right up and said:

"Hey, knock!
We know you like this knocking game,
But knock-knocks, do you have a name?"

And then a laugh we'd heard before
Laughed outside, inside our front door.
Mother smiled, and I did too,
Then Sinclair brought in Mom's lost shoe.

With both shoes on, she turned the knob.
Then Mom let out a little sob.
For standing there before our eyes,
The knockers yelled:

15

Aunts and uncles, cousins, friends
From our old town came pouring in.

"We came to stay for just the day.
We miss you since you moved away."

"But that's not all!" said Cousin Mabel.
"We brought food. Let's set the table!"

We could not believe our eyes
When we saw Grammy's berry pies.
And Uncle Floyd in his new suit
Brought bowls of pudding, bowls of fruit.

With Farmer Harden came my doubts.
"I brought some buttered brussels sprouts!
And something else I know we'll finish—
Bowls of my delicious spinach!"

"Don't worry," yelled Way Len and Reeze.
"We brought a pie with extra cheese!"

21

Lupé and her giant poodles
Whizzed right by with plates of noodles.

Mom's friend Tess and Grandpa Jake
Announced, "We baked a chocolate cake!"

23

Followed by Butcher Malone,
Who thought to bring Sinclair a bone.

Then suddenly we heard the feet
Of my twin cousins, Sam and Pete.
Pete and Sam and Sam and Pete
Ran in and yelled, "When do we eat?"

Squishing, squeezing 'round the table
Quickly set by Mom and Mabel.

Grammy, Grandpa, everyone
Eating, laughing, having fun.

But soon the clock struck half-past eight.
We all knew it was getting late.
Auntie Kate was first to say,
"We'll be back another day."

We hugged and hugged and hugged some more
Inside, outside our front door.
Wiping tears from both our eyes,
We thanked them for this big surprise.

We watched them drive into the night
And waved 'til they were out of sight.

Beneath the starry sky and moon,
We made a wish to see them soon.